EDGE BOOKS™

THE WORLD'S TOP TENS

THE WORLD'S
MOST DANGEROUS
JOBS

by Tim O'Shei

Capstone
press®

Mankato, Minnesota

Edge Books are published by Capstone Press,
151 Good Counsel Drive, P.O. Box 669, Mankato, Minnesota 56002.
www.capstonepress.com

Library of Congress Cataloging-in-Publication Data
O'Shei, Tim.
    The world's most dangerous jobs / by Tim O'Shei.
    p. cm.—(Edge books. The world's top tens)
    Includes bibliographical references and index.
    Summary: "Describes 10 of the world's most dangerous jobs in a countdown
format"—Provided by publisher.
    ISBN-13: 978-0-7368-6438-1 (hardcover)
    ISBN-10: 0-7368-6438-5 (hardcover)
    1. Hazardous occupations—Juvenile literature. I. Title. II. World's top tens
(Mankato, Minn.)
HD7262.O83 2007
331.7—dc22   2006003280

Editorial Credits
Angie Kaelberer, editor; Kate Opseth, set designer; PhaseOne, book designer; Wanda
    Winch, photo researcher; Scott Thoms, photo editor

Photo Credits
AccentAlaska.com/Tony Lara, 22, 27 (bottom left)
Corbis/Buena Vista Pictures/David Appleby, 13; David Turnley, 29; epa/Kai Forsterling, cover;
    Kevin Fleming, 24, 27 (bottom right); Leif Skoogfors, 10, 26 (bottom left); Paul A.
    Souders, 18, 27 (middle left); Reuters, 16, 27 (upper right); Rick Gayle, 6, 26 (upper left)
DVIC/SSGT Edward D. Holzapfel, USAF, 11
Getty Images Inc./AFP/Alexander Nemenov, 12, 26 (bottom right); Marco Garcia, 8, 26
    (upper right); Matthew Stockman, 4; Time Life Pictures/Taro Yamasaki, 19
Photri-MicroStock, 14, 27 (upper left)
SuperStock/age footstock, 21, 27 (middle right)

Capstone Press thanks the U.S. Bureau of Labor Statistics for reviewing this book. The Bureau of Labor
Statistics provides information on workers who are severely injured or killed on the job, including many of
the occupations found in this book. Measuring the most dangerous jobs is subjective. Some jobs employ
very few people (for example, elephant trainers); just one fatality or severe injury has a big effect. In a job
that employs many people, like police officers, there may be several fatalities or severe injuries, and yet the
overall effect is not as large. You can find out more about occupational injuries, illnesses, and fatalities from
the Bureau of Labor Statistics at http://www.bls.gov/iif.

1 2 3 4 5 6 11 10 09 08 07 06

TABLE OF

CONTENTS

DANGEROUS JOBS

Just inches separate race cars as drivers speed around the track. But even their job isn't dangerous enough to make our list.

Sliding down buildings. Leaping into fires. Balancing on metal beams hundreds of feet above the ground. Living with danger every day.

Exciting as these activities may sound, most people never do them. That's a good thing, because these tasks are dangerous. But for stunt doubles, smoke jumpers, Navy SEALs, and other daring workers, these adventures are part of everyday life. If these workers feel too safe, then they aren't doing their jobs!

10

People don't usually participate in high-speed crashes. Dummies are used instead.

TOP HUMAN TEST SPEED:	54 miles (87 kilometers) per hour
2004 U.S. CRASHES:	6.2 million; about 40,000 were fatal
FYI:	39 percent of all fatal crashes involve alcohol

HUMAN CRASH TEST DUMMY

Most drivers want to avoid car crashes. But not human crash test dummies. They smash and crash cars for a living.

Human crash test dummies are actually car accident reconstructionists. They study accidents by reenacting them. They drive off ramps, into poles, and into other cars.

Reconstructionist Rusty Haight has survived more than 700 crashes in cars, trucks, and school buses. Haight wears several sensors, which measure how his body reacts during the crash. He also wears kneepads, body armor, and a seat belt.

Haight uses his findings to teach police officers and others how and why injuries happen. His goal is to keep people safe.

9

ALSO CALLED: Fugitive recovery agents; bail enforcement agents

PAY: Ranges from a few hundred dollars to $1 million or more; they're only paid if they find and arrest the fugitive.

GENDER: About 40 percent are women

Bounty hunter Duane "Dog" Chapman (right) has his own TV show, *Dog the Bounty Hunter*.

BOUNTY HUNTER

Have you ever heard the saying, "out on bail"? A person charged with a crime must wait for the case to come to trial. Sometimes the person waits in jail. But judges often allow defendants to stay out of jail if they pay a large sum of money that guarantees they'll show up in court. This money is called a bail bond.

Defendants usually borrow the money from a bail bonding company. The company gets its money back when defendants show up in court. But some defendants run, becoming fugitives. That's where bounty hunters come in.

Bounty hunters find and arrest fugitives. Getting fugitives to open the door or talk on the phone can be tricky. Bounty hunters often pretend to be someone they are not. They might dress as delivery people or claim to be awarding prizes.

Once the fugitive is found, the job gets even harder. The bounty hunter has to arrest the fugitive, who may fight or run. Bounty hunters have to protect both themselves and any innocent bystanders.

The work of the armed forces is always dangerous, but the most deadly tasks go to the special forces. From parachuting in pitch-black darkness to blowing up terrorist camps, these soldiers do death-defying work.

Navy SEALs fight just as well in water as they do on land.

SPECIAL FORCES

SEAL NAME:	Stands for Sea, Air, and Land
GREEN BERETS NAME:	Comes from the soldiers' dark green hats
DELTA FORCE FOUNDER:	Colonel Charlie Beckwith

The 10th Special Forces Group is part of the Green Berets.

Navy SEALs are trained to fight on land, in water, and in the air. They are weapons experts, skilled scuba divers, and experienced paratroopers.

Army Special Forces soldiers are known as Green Berets. Two of their main missions are fighting terrorists and spying on enemy forces and governments. They often live undercover in other countries.

The Army's 1st Special Forces Operational Detachment is called Delta Force. It formed in 1977 to fight terrorist groups. Delta Force is so secretive that the government doesn't even admit it exists.

7. STUNT DOUBLE

Some stunt doubles specialize in car stunts.

SKILLS:	Rappelling, martial arts, and expert driving
MOST COMMON SCENES:	Fight scenes
FAMOUS STUNT DOUBLES:	Dar Robinson, Bob Yerkes

Jackie Chan did his own stunts in the movie *Around the World in 80 Days*.

Movie fans love fiery explosions, ferocious fights, and daring rescues. Creating those scenes can be risky. That's why moviemakers hire stunt doubles to set up and perform death-defying scenes.

On a TV or movie set, the director describes what an action scene should look like. The stunt double figures out the safest way to perform the scene while still making it look real. Then, the double teaches the actor how to do the scene. But if the job is too dangerous, the double takes over.

Some actors, like Jackie Chan, do their own stunts. Chan's riskiest stunt was in the 1998 movie *Who Am I?* His character fights bad guys on top of a 21-story building. To escape, he slides down the side of the building to the sidewalk!

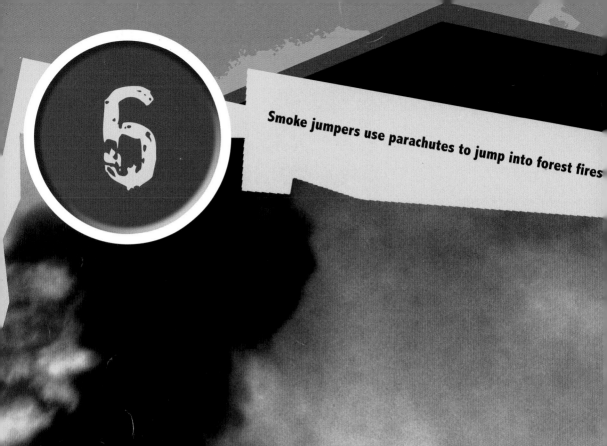

6

Smoke jumpers use parachutes to jump into forest fires

FIRST SMOKE JUMP:	July 12, 1940
EMPLOYERS:	U.S. Forest Service and the Bureau of Land Management
WORK SEASON:	About June 1 to November 1
STARTING WAGE:	$13 per hour in 2005

SMOKE JUMPER

A bolt of lightning strikes a tree. Branches split, flames burst outward, and smoke spews into the air. Soon, another tree is on fire, and then another. Before long, a fire rages through the forest.

Most people would flee from this red-hot mess. But a special group of firefighters flock to the flames.

Smoke jumpers are firefighters who use parachutes to jump from planes into burning forests. Ground vehicles often can't reach these areas. The smoke jumpers' mission is to stop the fire while it's still small.

At the fire site, jumpers quickly get to work with chain saws, axes, and shovels. They trim branches and chop down trees to stop the fire from spreading. If the fire has nothing to burn, it will often die out. Sometimes, jumpers use explosives to clear larger areas. As they work, they risk being trapped by flames or injured by falling trees. Since 1940, at least 30 smoke jumpers have died in the line of duty.

5

SWAT officers sometimes use armored vehicles.

EQUIPMENT: Fireproof clothing, bulletproof vests, high-powered binoculars, armored vehicles, and night vision goggles

WEAPONS: Assault rifles, sniper rifles, submachine guns, tear gas grenades

SWAT OFFICER

It's lunchtime inside a busy restaurant, but no one is eating. Every customer and worker is frozen in fear. A gunman is holding everyone in the restaurant hostage.

This situation calls for a Special Weapons and Tactics (SWAT) team. SWAT officers are highly trained fighters who are as fit as superstar athletes.

The first SWAT teams formed in California during the 1960s. Today, SWAT teams are found in cities around the world.

In a situation like the one above, officers would surround the restaurant. Marksmen would look for a clear shot at the gunman. Another team member would try to convince the gunman to release the hostages.

If the gunman shoots, the team enters the building. The marksmen may shoot back at the gunman, but only if they can do it safely. A team's top goal is to keep the public safe.

4

Farms look peaceful and relaxing, but dangers lurk behind those green fields and grazing animals.

Farmers work long hours, and they often work alone. Such hard outdoor work can be life threatening. In July 2005, three farm

Hands can easily get caught in machinery blades.

FARM WORKER

U.S. DEATHS: 646 in 2004

AGES: Many farm injuries involve children, who often operate machinery and work with animals.

FYI: About half of all farm-related deaths involve vehicles and other machinery.

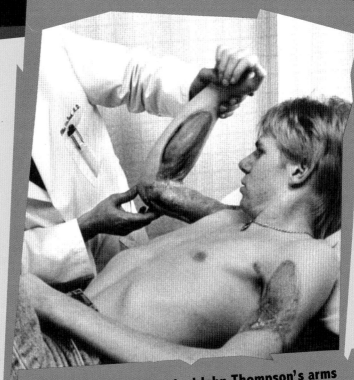

In 1992, doctors reattached John Thompson's arms after they were pulled off by a farm machine.

workers in California died in 100-degree Fahrenheit (38-degree Celsius) temperatures.

Weather isn't the only dangerous factor. Farmers operate heavy equipment with massive, swinging blades. Accidents can be deadly. Equipment can roll over onto people. Body parts can get caught in cutting equipment. Farmers also work with powerful chemicals used in fertilizers and pesticides. These chemicals can cause cancer and respiratory diseases.

3

No construction job is safe, but building skyscrapers is especially dangerous. The people who build these massive towers are called structured metal workers.

Structured metal workers are constantly in danger of falling. Workers wear belts attached to harnesses. Nets also help keep them safe. Still, the workers are hundreds of feet above ground, dealing with heavy pieces of steel. They work outside in both hot and cold weather. Under those conditions, workers' lives are always at risk.

At a construction site, workers receive stacks of steel beams that weigh thousands of pounds. Cranes lift the steel into the air. One worker directs the crane operator. Another grasps a rope attached to the steel to keep it steady. More workers wait up high. They carefully position the steel and fasten it in place.

Structured metal workers rely on teamwork and trust. They work carefully and communicate clearly. If everything goes according to plan, their jobs are safe. But simple trips or slips can be deadly.

STRUCTURED METAL WORKER

ALSO CALLED:	Ironworkers, even though they usually work with steel
DEATHS:	47 per 100,000 workers in 2004
MEDIAN WAGE:	$20.40 per hour in 2004

Structured metal workers balance on narrow steel beams high above the ground.

2

Crab fishermen fight cold winds and high waves as they load the day's catch.

KING CRAB SIZE:	Up to 18 pounds (8.2 kilograms)
TYPES:	Red king crabs, blue king crabs, and snow crabs
AVERAGE PRICE:	$4.70 per pound of crab in 2004
INJURY RATE:	Almost 100% during fishing season

CRAB FISHERMAN

One of the world's most dangerous jobs is also one of the world's shortest jobs. Alaskan crab fishermen work only a few weeks a year. But they are paid well for their time. Some earn $1,000 each day.

Twice each year, usually in October and January, about 200 boats travel to the Bering Sea off the coast of Alaska. Each boat carries crab pots, which are 700-pound (318-kilogram) tanks. Fishermen fill the pots with bait and lower them 400 feet (122 meters) to the bottom of the sea.

Why is this so dangerous? The weather is nasty, with high winds and freezing temperatures. To catch as many crabs as possible, fishermen often work 20 hours straight. Injuries are common. Many fishermen break fingers or ribs. The heavy crab pots sometimes fall on fishermen or knock them down.

In 2005, the state Board of Fisheries tried to make crab fishing safer. The board gave each boat a crab quota. Fishermen no longer have to rush to catch as many crabs as possible before the season closes. But some fishermen worry they will earn less money under the new rule.

1

Loggers plan how each tree will fall. But sometimes, the tree doesn't follow that plan.

LOCATIONS:	Western and southeastern United States
DEATHS:	92 per 100,000 workers in 2004
MEDIAN WAGE:	$14.29 per hour in 2004
RATING:	Most dangerous U.S. job, according to the Occupational Safety and Health Administration (OSHA)

LOGGER

In the middle of a forest, a group of men stand near a large tree. One man cuts a large notch in the tree's trunk with a chain saw. Two more swipes of the chain saw, and the tree is ready to fall. The loggers grab their chain saws and scramble to safety. Once the tree is on the ground, they cut off the branches and saw the trunk into logs.

Loggers cut trees for lumber and paper. They also clear land for roads or buildings. They use axes and chain saws to cut down trees. Tractors and skidders help them pull away logs.

Forests have lots of surprises like buried roots, slippery ground, and wild animals. With those dangers, along with all that sharp, heavy equipment, loggers must always be careful. Loggers know how to control the direction of a falling tree, but there are no guarantees the fall will go as planned. Any small mistake can be deadly.

The World's Most Dangerous JOBS

10

HUMAN CRASH TEST DUMMY

9

BOUNTY HUNTER

8

SPECIAL FORCES

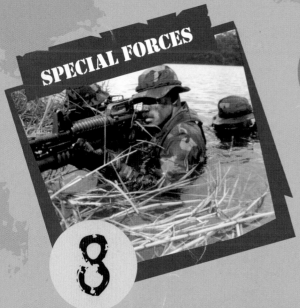

7

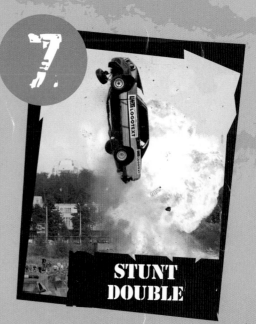

STUNT DOUBLE

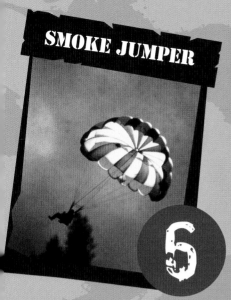

SMOKE JUMPER

6

SWAT OFFICER

5

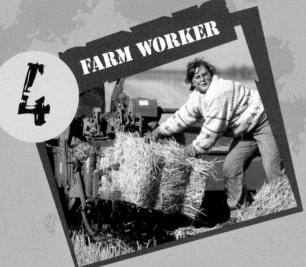

FARM WORKER

4

STRUCTURED METAL WORKER

3

CRAB FISHERMAN

2

LOGGER

1

UNDERSTANDING DANGEROUS JOBS

Danger is real. So are the people who face it every day.

People eat delicious meals of crab, caught by fishermen who endure the coldest, nastiest weather on the planet. People walk city streets kept safe by police officers. People work in offices built by workers who move heavy metal beams hundreds of feet above the ground.

Workers with dangerous jobs have amazing skills. In most cases, they also have many years of training. That's why no one should copy them. For someone who doesn't know how to do it, a dangerous job can quickly become a deadly one.

Every day, firefighters and other workers risk their lives.

Glossary

defendant (di-FEN-duhnt)—the person in a court case who may have broken a law or caused a legal problem

fugitive (FYOO-juh-tiv)—a person charged with a crime who runs away from the law

hostage (HOSS-tij)—a person held against his or her will

parachute (PA-ruh-shoot)—a large piece of strong, lightweight fabric; parachutes allow people to jump from high places and float slowly and safely to the ground.

quota (KWOH-tuh)—a fixed number or share of something

rappel (ruh-PEL)—to slide down a strong rope

reconstructionist (ree-kuhn-STRUHK-shuh-nist)—a person who recreates car crashes to find out how and why they happened

Read More

Briscoe, Diana. *Smokejumpers: Battling the Forest Flames.* High Five Reading. Mankato, Minn.: Capstone Press, 2003.

Cefrey, Holly. *Bounty Hunter.* Danger Is My Business. New York: Children's Press, 2003.

Hamilton, John. *Special Forces.* Defending the Nation. Edina, Minn.: Abdo, 2006.

Hyland, Tony. *Stunt Performers.* Extreme Jobs. North Mankato, Minn.: Smart Apple, 2006.

Internet Sites

FactHound offers a safe, fun way to find Internet sites related to this book. All of the sites on FactHound have been researched by our staff.

Here's how:

1. Visit *www.facthound.com*
2. Choose your grade level.
3. Type in this book ID **0736864385** for age-appropriate sites. You may also browse subjects by clicking on letters, or by clicking on pictures and words.
4. Click on the **Fetch It** button.

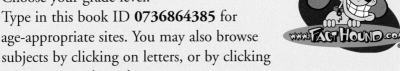

FactHound will fetch the best sites for you!

INDEX